First published: August 1, 2015

ISBN: HC 78-1-943413-00-3
ISBN: SC 78-1-943413-01-0

Visit us on the web!
www.tozknows.com

In addition to promoting literacy and biblical education to children, Toz Knows partners with non-profit and other charity organizations to give back to the community. For every TWO Toz Knows books purchased, ONE is donated to a child in need.

For more information regarding a partnership with Toz Knows, visit
www.tozknows.com/partners

Printed in the United States of America

Illustrator: Tina Modugno
www.tinamodugno.com

Toz Knows

The Paralytic Friend

Mindi Jo Furby & Kristin Lee Arnold

Illustrated by Tina Modugno

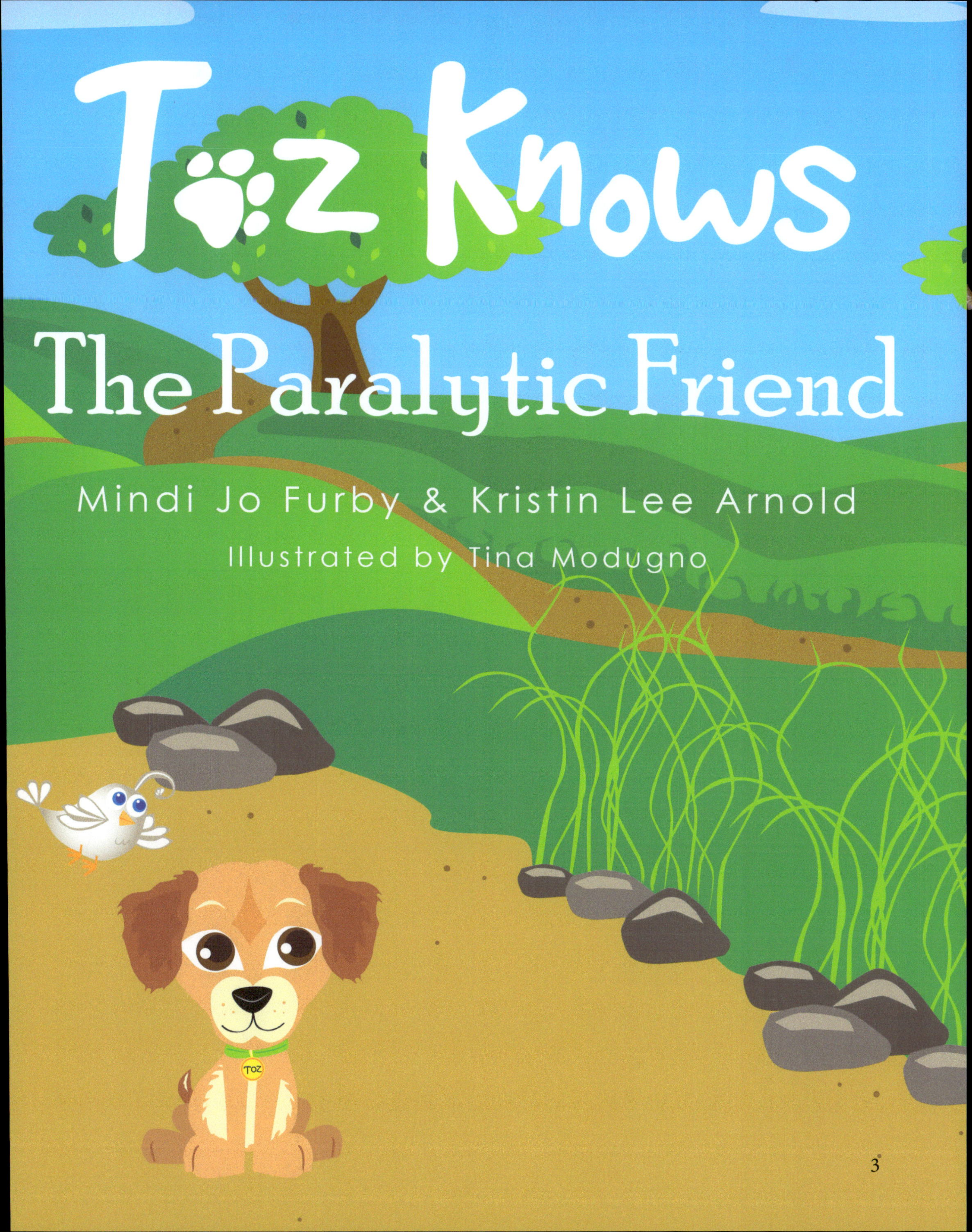

The Paralytic Friend
Mark 2:1-12 (NIV)

A few days later, when Jesus again entered Capernaum, the people heard that he had come home. They gathered in such large numbers that there was no room left, not even outside the door, and he preached the word to them. Some men came, bringing to him a paralyzed man, carried by four of them. Since they could not get him to Jesus because of the crowd, they made an opening in the roof above Jesus by digging through it and then lowered the mat the man was lying on. When Jesus saw their faith, he said to the paralyzed man, "Son, your sins are forgiven." Now some teachers of the law were sitting there, thinking to themselves, "Why does this fellow talk like that? He's blaspheming! Who can forgive sins but God alone?"

Immediately Jesus knew in his spirit that this was what they were thinking in their hearts, and he said to them, "Why are you thinking these things? Which is easier: to say to this paralyzed man, 'Your sins are forgiven,' or to say, 'Get up, take your mat and walk'? But I want you to know that the Son of Man has authority on earth to forgive sins." So he said to the man, "I tell you, get up, take your mat and go home." He got up, took his mat and walked out in full view of them all. This amazed everyone and they praised God, saying, "We have never seen anything like this!"

It was your typical sunny day.
Moms and dads working,
Sounds of birds chirping,
Little ones happily laughing at play.

Litters of pups—
Purebreds and mutts,
Kittens galore,
Critters from the shore,
Stingrays and bees
Playing as they please!

Soaring through the air
Was the White Bird with a smile,
Looking down at a pile
Of the many toys they shared.

Woody and Toz,
Pawing and pulling,
Running and rolling,
Away they go!

"Hey pals! Wait for me!"
said sweet Miss Miley.
Quickly she galloped,
Past the sea scallops,
Toward her buddies,
Tozer and Woody.

The three little ones
Skipped down the shore
Laughed more and more
Having loads of fun.

9

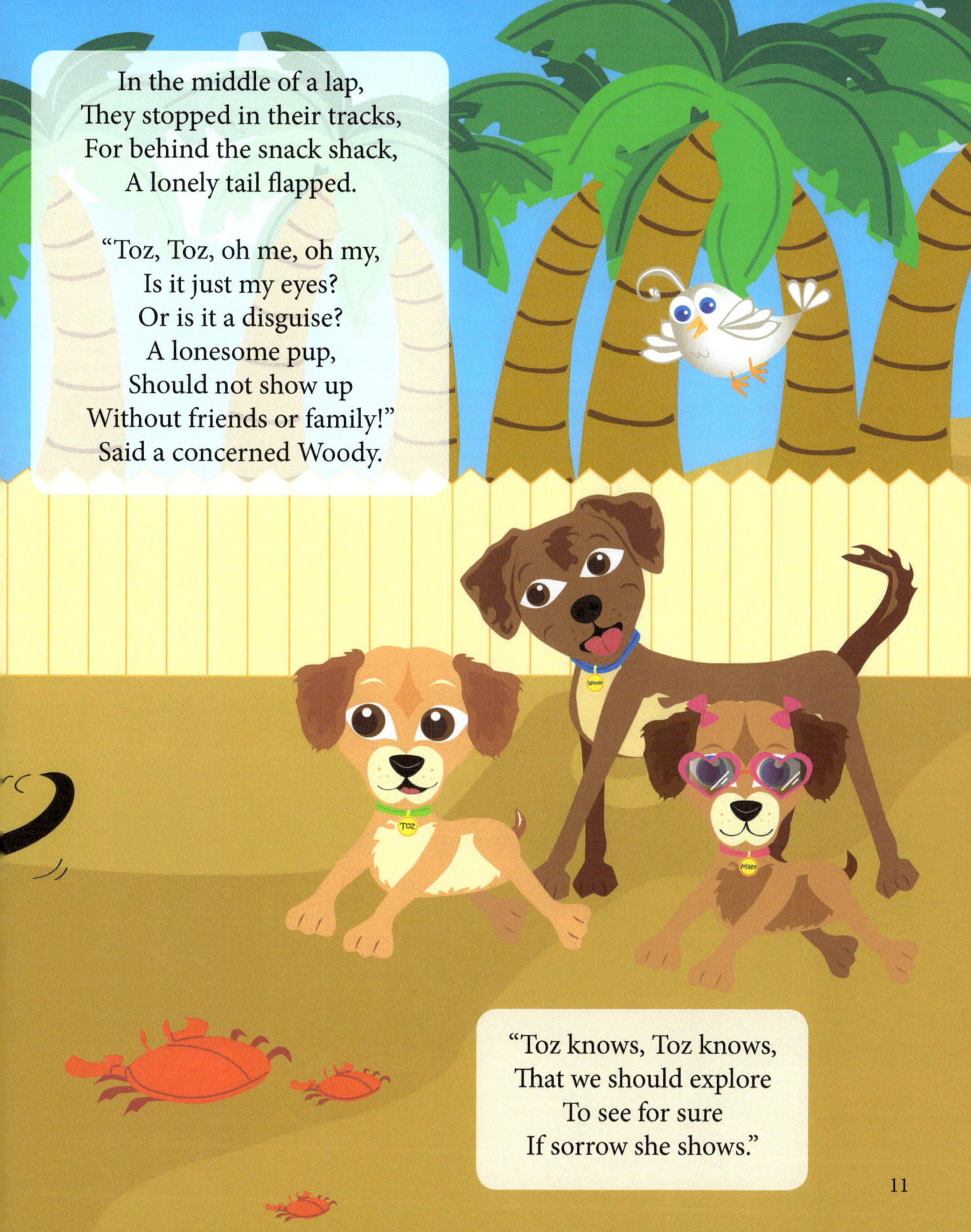

In the middle of a lap,
They stopped in their tracks,
For behind the snack shack,
A lonely tail flapped.

"Toz, Toz, oh me, oh my,
Is it just my eyes?
Or is it a disguise?
A lonesome pup,
Should not show up
Without friends or family!"
Said a concerned Woody.

"Toz knows, Toz knows,
That we should explore
To see for sure
If sorrow she shows."

"But wait," paused Miley.
"Is this a good choice?"
"Of course!" Chimed Woody's voice.
"You just wait and see!"

"Do you hear her yelps?
She may need some help!
Toz knows, Toz knows,
That the past shows,
It is important to help others,
Even those not our brothers."

Tozer and his buds,
Crept slowly like snails
Towards the friendless tail,
Wagging with soft thuds.

"Hi pal, my name is Toz.
This is Woody and Miley,
What a great day at Tybee!
How does it go?"

"Oh, I've had better days,
For now I am in pain
That won't go away.
My friends have strayed,
I can't walk or play."
Cried Mackey as she lay.

Tozer, filled with dread,
Looked up to the sky,
Saw the White Bird fly by,
And heard Him in his head.

"Think back to the story
About a disabled man,
Whom I gave a hand,
To display My Glory.
His friends stayed beside him,
Making things seem less grim."

Toz racked his brain
Again and again,
Until he recalled,
The story in all…

A long time ago,
The world did not show
Many signs of our God—
Things then were quite flawed.

But then word got around
Spreading town to town,
Of a Man who lived,
To forgive every sin.
He did lots of good deeds
And healed those in need.

From land to land,
He went to aid,
And teach and pray
Fulfilling the plan!

One day His hometown stirred.
"Let's go, Jesus is here!"
"The house He's in is near!"
Everyone ran in a blur.

Four men decided to send
Their friend who needed to mend.
The paralysis kept him sitting
He couldn't walk, his body quitting.

Getting ready,
They grabbed a mat
And laid him flat
To keep him steady.

Onward they went
Carrying their pal
Around and around
Until they were spent.

Once they arrived,
All four men sighed
With lots of relief.
They could not believe
This exciting day.
Hip hip hooray!

"Oh me oh my,
People everywhere,
Far, near, here, there,
What a sight!"

"What are we to do?
There's no room!
Oh, what gloom!
Not an inch,
Nor a pinch!"
Said friend, number two.

"We came all this way,
We are here to stay!"
Said friend number three,
As his eyes held a gleam.

As they followed his eyes
His friends soon caught on,
Their frustrations gone.
To the roof they'd climb!

Their belief was so strong,
To Jesus, their hearts belonged.

They climbed up with might,
Oh, what a sight!
Their dedication was clear,
Their friendship was dear.

Through the clay and reeds
That covered the roof top,
Lay a spot they could drop
Their friend to Him,
Who preached within
And could help indeed!

They dug and dug
Through the yuck,
Under the muck,
Although folks looked real smug.

They were getting near
And began to hear
The excitement below
As the chatter did grow.

29

From a hole in the thatch
Their paralytic friend went
Down, tired, and spent
On his little mat.

Oh, what a sight,
This man in flight,
Coming down and down
Right to the ground!

Their faith in Him
Was near and dear,
Jesus' decision was clear,
He said, "You're forgiven!"

Those who didn't believe
Could never see
That within His words
Were power and cures.

Their hearts stayed cold
Their disrespect bold.

"Get up!" Jesus cried,
"And walk on out.
Go ahead, turn about!"
He decided to try!

The disabled man
Then stood upright,
And with all his might
Walked out of sight,
Without a helping hand.

"Whoa, earth to Toz!"
Woody quacked
Snapping Toz back.
"Where did you go?
What does Toz know?"

"Toz knows, Toz knows,
That we must lend
A helping hand
To our new friend,
And help her mend;
We'll take it slow."

"In time we'll see
That friendly Mackey
Might soon one day
Be able to play!"

37

With an open mind,
And hearts so big,
The pups let in
A new pal, how kind!

The White Bird up high
Kept a watchful eye,
As He flew on by
In the beautiful sky.

Happy He was to see
How Toz and his crew
Befriended someone new,
Who was viewed differently.

Mackey's disability
Would not get in the way
Of joyful noise and play
Day after day, happily.

MEET THE TEAM!

Mindi Jo Furby
Co-Author / Publicist

Mindi Jo Furby is an author and speaker who decicates her life to fighting biblical illiteracy one publication at a time. Equipped with a degree in Biblical Studies and a Masters in Religion, she loves helping others fall in love with God through the pages of His Word. She, her husband, daughter and pups make their home near Hilton Head, SC.

www.mindijofurby.com

Kristin Lee Arnold
Co-Author

Kristin Lee Arnold is a UNC Chapel Hill grad who's pursuing her Masters in Special Education at Armstrong University. She loves children and has an incredible talent for writing books that not only entertain, but teach them truths about life and God in new and exciting ways! She makes her home in Savannah, GA, along with her pup, Woody.

Kaci Ann Hollingsworth
Non-Profit Coordinator

Kaci Ann Hollingsworth is also a UNC Chapel Hill grad who loves non-profit organizations and initiatives. She currently works for a non-profit and volunteers with many others. She makes her home with her pup, Mackey, in Hilton Head Island, SC.

Tina Modugno
Children's Illustrator

Tina Modugno is an illustrator, author and publicist from Quebec, Canada. She has illustrated and published many titles including some of her own children's books. Tina is a huge animal advocate and lives with five feline family members. She is the creator of *"The Oreo Cat"* and through her work, she is dedicated to helping educate the public about the crippling side effects of feline declawing.

www.tinamodugno.com
www.theoreocat.com